For my big brother "Edurd" who taught me so much about the
outdoors and all the gifts our animal relatives give us — N.C.

To Maria & Mino, my new family. I love you with all my heart — J.M.P.S.

ACKNOWLEDGMENTS

I'd like to thank the women who helped me with the translations in this book: Estelle Amikons,
Janice Brant, Taqralik Partridge, Jamie Metallic, Koosen Pielle, and Maria Campbell.

Owlkids Books gratefully acknowledges that our office in Toronto is located on the traditional territory of many nations, including
the Mississaugas of the Credit, the Chippewa, the Wendat, the Anishinaabeg, and the Haudenosaunee Peoples.

Owlkids Books acknowledges the financial support of the Canada Council for the Arts, the Ontario Arts Council, the Government of Canada
through the Canada Book Fund (CBF) and the Government of Ontario through the Ontario Creates Book Initiative for our publishing activities.

A version of this story appeared as "Amik's Big Day" in the April 2021 issue of *Chirp* magazine.

Published in Canada by Owlkids Books Inc., 1 Eglinton Avenue East, Toronto, ON M4P 3A1 | Published in the US by Owlkids Books Inc., 1700 Fourth Street, Berkeley, CA 94710

Library of Congress Control Number: 2022939094

LIBRARY AND ARCHIVES CANADA CATALOGUING IN PUBLICATION

Title: Biindigen! : Amik says welcome / Nancy Cooper ; illustrated by Joshua Mangeshig Pawis-Steckley.
Other titles: Amik says welcome
Names: Cooper, Nancy, 1967- author. | Pawis-Steckley, Joshua Mangeshig, illustrator.
Identifiers: Canadiana 20220250766 | ISBN 9781771475150 (hardcover)
Subjects: LCGFT: Picture books.
Classification: LCC PS8605.O6713 B55 2023 | DDC jC813/.6—dc23

Edited by Jennifer Stokes | Designed by Elisa Gutiérrez

Manufactured in Guangdong Province, Dongguan City, China, in August 2022, by Toppan Leefung
Packaging & Printing (Dongguan) Co., Ltd. Job #BAYDC110

A   B   C   D   E   F

ONTARIO ARTS COUNCIL
CONSEIL DES ARTS DE L'ONTARIO
an Ontario government agency
un organisme du gouvernement de l'Ontario

Canada Council
for the Arts

Conseil des Arts
du Canada

Canadä

Publisher of Chirp, Chickadee and OWL
www.owlkidsbooks.com | Owlkids Books is a division of bayard canada

FSC MIX
Paper from
responsible sources
FSC® C104723

Biindigen!
Amik Says Welcome

NANCY COOPER

illustrated by

JOSHUA MANGESHIG PAWIS-STECKLEY

OWLKIDS BOOKS

Amik hears a slapping sound and sees ripples in the water.

They're coming!

Today, Amik's cousins are visiting her lodge. They're coming from all over the forest, and she has so much to show them!

Amik's little sister, Nishiime, is so excited she can't keep still. She's also nervous.

"What will they be like?" she asks Amik. "Will they be the same as us?"

Amisk, who lives close by, is the first to arrive.
Then Gopit and Amicos show up from the East.
Qowut from the far West.
And Kigiaq from the North.

Last to arrive is Tsyennìto from the South—and he is out of breath!

"Sorry I was late," says Tsyennìto. "I was frightened by a huge bear along the shore! I flapped my tail to warn you. Did you hear?"

"Thanks for the warning," Amik says, "but don't be afraid. The bear is just looking in the water for insects and plant roots. She likes that we dam the stream, making shallow areas for her and her cubs."

To start the visit, the cousins thank Amik for having them on her territory and invite her to visit theirs one day. They have each brought a gift to share.

Amisk brought some dried muskeg tea.

Gopit brought a birchbark basket filled with wild strawberries.

Amicos brought some juicy maple twigs.

Qowut brought a woven
cedar headband.

Kigiaq brought
dried crowberries.

And Tsyennìto brought
a small purple wampum
shell that fits perfectly in
Amik's paw.

Amik turns to introduce Nishiime
to the cousins—but she's gone!
Amik calls and calls, but Nishiime
is nowhere to be found.

Amik and her cousins head to the family lodge to look for Nishiime and meet Amik's parents, who are cutting down a poplar tree. While the beavers visit, two white-tailed deer come out of the forest to nibble on the poplar leaves.

"Miigwech," says one deer to the beavers. "It's easier for us to get to these leaves after you cut down the trees."

"Excuse me, Waawaashkeshi," Amik asks the deer. "Have you seen my little sister?"

"No," Waawaashkeshi replies. "We've been busy foraging for buds and twigs."

As Amik and her cousins swim away from the lodge, they see flashes of silver and gold in the water beneath them. It's tiny fish swimming through deep canals that the beavers dug into the mud.

"Miigwech," one fish says to the beavers. "No matter how thick the winter ice gets, we always have water to swim in because of these canals."

"Excuse me, Giigoonh," Amik asks the fish. "Have you seen my little sister?"

"No," Giigoonh replies. "We've been busy eating bugs."

After a short swim, the group of beavers reaches one of Amik's family's dams. They climb onto the dam just after a red fox runs across it.

The cousins are afraid, but Amik says, "This is my friend Waagosh."

"Miigwech," the fox says. "Being able to run across this dam helps me get quickly home to my family."

"Excuse me, Waagosh," Amik asks the fox. "Have you seen my little sister?"

"No," Waagosh replies. "I've been busy hunting for my family's dinner."

The beavers look down over the dam to the field below. A mother otter is there with her babies, playing in the shallow water. "Miigwech," says the otter mother. "I teach my kits to feed themselves in these shallow streams made by your dam. They're learning to hunt minnows and tadpoles."

"Excuse me, Nigig," Amik asks
the otter. "Have you seen my little
sister?"

"No," says Nigig. "We've been
busy catching tadpoles."

The sun is starting to head west, and the shadows are getting longer. It's time for the visit to end.

Amik wonders where her sister has been all this time. Nishiime had been so excited to meet her cousins from far away.

Just then, Amik feels a scratch on her back. She twists around and sees Nishiime.

"Where have you been?" asks Amik. "You missed the whole visit!"

"I hid," says Nishiime. "I was scared to meet other beavers."

"What made you come out of hiding?" asks Amik.

"I watched you from the trees, and I could see that our cousins are just like us, even though they live far away and have different families."

Amik introduces Nishiime to their cousins, and she is full of questions.

Her cousins tell Nishiime about where they live and what it's like on their ponds and streams.

"Could I come and visit you when I'm older?" she asks.

"Yes!" the cousins reply.

As dusk settles over the forest, the cousins slip into
the stream and head back to their homes.

One day they will all grow up and have their own
families. And Amik knows they will teach their babies
that beavers are an important part of Creation.

TRANSLATION OF ANISHINAABE WORDS

biindigen [**been**-dih-gen]: welcome

giigoonh [ghee-**goh**]: fish

miigwetch [**mee**-gwech]: thank you

nigig [nih-**gig**]: otter

nishiime [nih-**shee**-may]: younger sister

waagosh [wah-**gosh**]: fox

waawaashkeshi [wah-wash-**kay**-shih]: deer

baa maa pii [bah mah pee]: until later

Each beaver in the story comes from a different Nation, and their names mean "beaver" in their own language:

Amik [**ah**-mik]
(Anishinaabe)

Amisk [**ah**-misk]
(Cree)

Gopit [**go**-bit]
(Mi'kmaq)

Amicos [**ah**-mi-kos]
(Algonquin)

Kigiaq [**kee**-ghee-ack]
(Inuktitut)

Qowut [k'oh-woot]
(Ayajuthum)

Tsyennìto [ja-**nee**-doh]
(Kanyen'kéha Mohawk)

Baa maa pii!